NICK BUTTERWORTH'S BOOK OF NURSERY RHYMES

To Allison   10/15/91
From
Jan & Brad Dolgin

VIKING

VIKING
Published by the Penguin Group
Viking Penguin, a division of Penguin Books USA Inc.,
375 Hudson Street, New York, New York 10014, U.S.A.
Penguin Books Australia Ltd, Ringwood, Victoria, Australia
Penguin Books Canada Ltd, 2801 John Street, Markham, Ontario, Canada L3R 1B4
Penguin Books (N.Z.) Ltd, 182-190 Wairau Road, Auckland 10, New Zealand

First published in Great Britain by MacDonald & Co. 1981
This edition published in Great Britain by Aurum Books for Children 1990
First American edition published 1991

10　9　8　7　6　5　4　3　2　1

Library of Congress Catalog Card Number 90-50129
ISBN: 0-670-83551-X

Printed and bound in Italy

CONTENTS

ary had a little lamb,
  Its fleece was white as snow;
  And everywhere that Mary went
The lamb was sure to go.

It followed her to school one day,
That was against the rule;
It made the children laugh and play
To see a lamb at school.

The north wind doth blow,
    And we shall have snow,
And what will poor robin do then?
Poor thing.

He'll sit in the barn
And keep himself warm,
And hide his head under his wing.
Poor thing.

Jack and Jill went up the hill
 To fetch a pail of water;
 Jack fell down and broke his crown,
And Jill came tumbling after.

Up Jack got, and home did trot,
As fast as he could caper;
He went to bed to mend his head
With vinegar and brown paper.

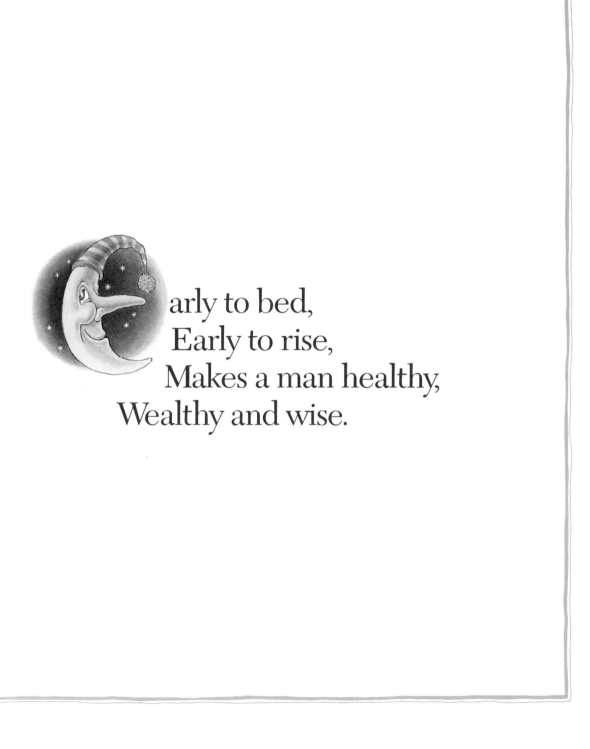arly to bed,
Early to rise,
Makes a man healthy,
Wealthy and wise.

THere was an old woman
    Who lived in a shoe,
      She had so many children
She didn't know what to do;
She gave them some broth
Without any bread;
Then whipped them all soundly
And put them to bed.

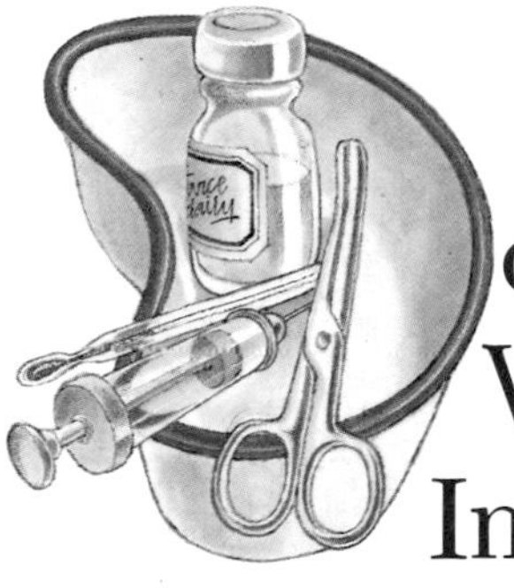

octor Foster
Went to Gloucester
In a shower of rain;
He stepped in a puddle,
Right up to his middle,
And never went there again.

umpty Dumpty,
sat on a wall;
Humpty Dumpty
had a great fall.
All the king's horses,
  and all the king's men,
Couldn't put Humpty
  together again.

To market, to market,
    To buy a fat pig;
Home again, home again,
Jiggety jig.

To market, to market,
To buy a fat hog;
Home again, home again,
Joggety jog.

Three blind mice,
   Three blind mice,
      See how they run!
   See how they run!
They all ran after
   the farmer's wife,
Who cut off their tails
   with a carving knife,
Did you ever see
   such a thing in your life
As three blind mice?

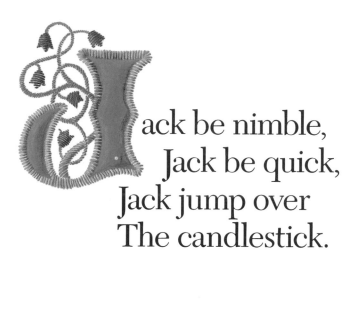

Jack be nimble,
    Jack be quick,
Jack jump over
The candlestick.

ittle Bo Peep has lost her sheep,
   And can't tell where
     to find them;
Leave them alone,
   and they'll come home,
Bringing their tails behind them.

Can you find six sheep hiding in the picture?

Wee Willie Winkie
  Runs through the town,
  Upstairs and downstairs
In his nightgown;
Rapping at the window,
Crying through the lock,
Are the children in their beds?
It's past eight o'clock!

Baa, baa, black sheep,
Have you any wool?
Yes sir, yes sir,
Three bags full;
One for the master,
And one for the dame,
And one for the little boy
Who lives down the lane.

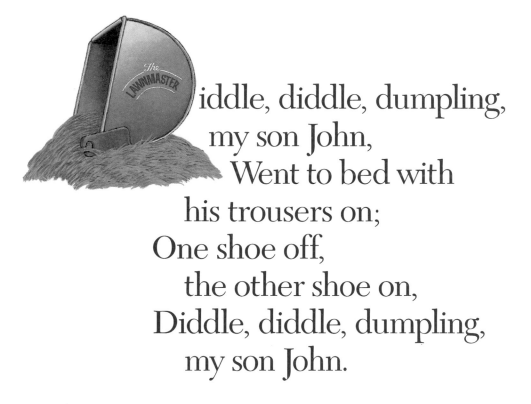Diddle, diddle, dumpling,
my son John,
Went to bed with
his trousers on;
One shoe off,
the other shoe on,
Diddle, diddle, dumpling,
my son John.

ickory, dickory, dock,
The mouse ran up the clock.
The clock struck one,
The mouse ran down,
Hickory, dickory, dock.

ncey Wincey spider
　　Climbed the water spout;
　　Down came the rain and
Washed the spider out.
Out came the sun and
Dried up all the rain;
Incey Wincey spider
Climbed up the spout again.

olly put the kettle on,
Polly put the kettle on,
Polly put the kettle on,
We'll all have tea.

Sukey take it off again,
Sukey take it off again,
Sukey take it off again,
They've all gone away.

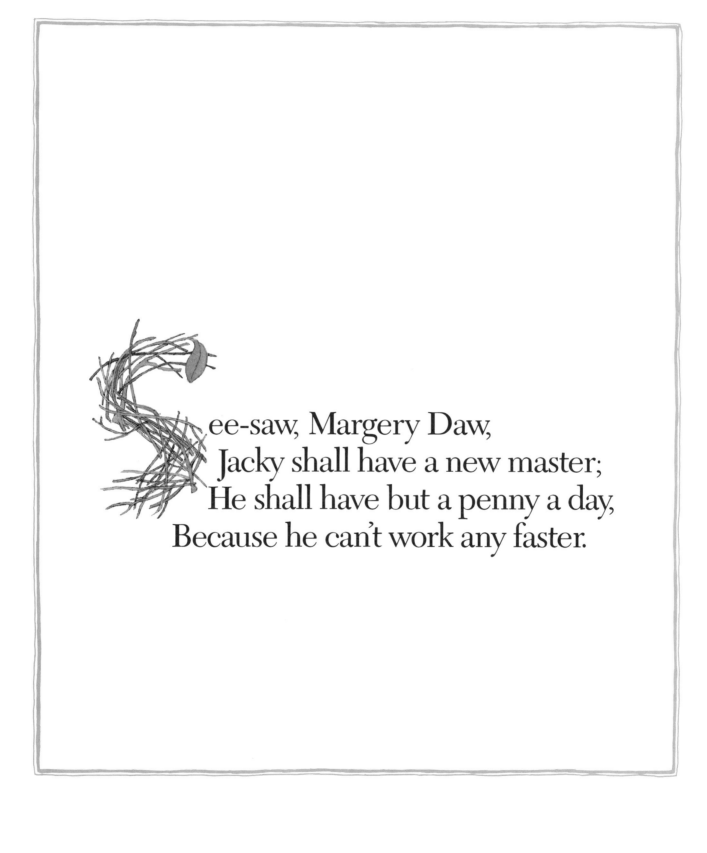

See-saw, Margery Daw,
Jacky shall have a new master;
He shall have but a penny a day,
Because he can't work any faster.

ussy cat, pussy cat,
Where have you been?
I've been to London
To look at the Queen.

Pussy cat, pussy cat,
What did you there?
I frightened a little mouse
Under her chair.

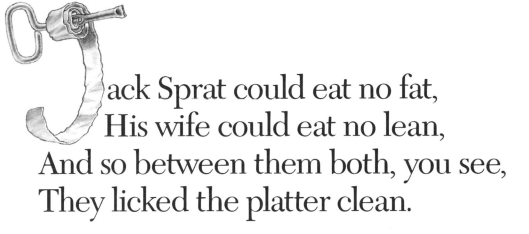

Jack Sprat could eat no fat,
His wife could eat no lean,
And so between them both, you see,
They licked the platter clean.

ey diddle diddle,
The cat and the fiddle,
The cow jumped over
the moon;
The little dog laughed
To see such sport,
And the dish ran away
with the spoon.

Twinkle, twinkle, little star,
How I wonder what you are!
Up above the world so high,
Like a diamond in the sky.

When the blazing sun is gone,
When he nothing shines upon,
Then you show your little light,
Twinkle, twinkle, all the night.

Then the traveller in the dark,
Thanks you for your tiny spark,
He could not tell which way to go,
If you did not twinkle so.